The Mucky Princess

and The Rouge of Revenge

By Richard Cleveland
Illustrated by Matthew Cleveland

Book 3
of the Mucky Princess series

About the Author

Richard Cleveland was born in Enfield, North London in 1950.
After leaving a local grammar school, he trained as a teacher of English and History St.Mark and St. John College in Chelsea. In a teaching career of forty years taught at a number of secondary schools in North and East London and later became a teacher of Geography and is a Fellow of the Royal Geographical Society. He is married to Geraldine and they have three sons and two grandchildren. After retirement he took up beekeeping and writing stories for his grandchildren of which the Mucky Princess is one.

Acknowledgement

This book would not have been possible without the help and support from the following people:

Sophie and Oliver Cleveland, Abigail and Emily Thornton, Lidia Oliver, Isabelle Featherstone and the staff and children of Gaelscoil O'Doghair, Limerick, Eire.

Contact:

info@themuckyprincess

www.themuckyprincess.com

For Sophie and Oliver

Other books in the series:

The Mucky Princess

The Mucky Princess and the Lipstick of Truth

Coming Soon:

Narvig the Nobbly Gnome of the North

The Anti-Santa

Visit:

www.themuckyprincess.com

The Mucky Princess and the Rouge of Revenge

CHAPTER ONE

Once upon a time, in some high mountains just far enough away from you and me that we can only see them if we really look hard and squeeze the very last bit out of our imagination, there sat the Wicked Queen.

I say the Wicked Queen, but really she was the Wicked Ex-Queen who had been banished far, far away by her husband, the king, because the much loved, and not at all wicked, Mucky Princess had tricked her into confessing that it was she who had given his first queen a poison apple. She had then cast a spell on his son that made him look very much like a horse and his long teeth made it hard for him say his Rs and he soon became known as the pwince.

The king was convinced that his son had a terrible and infectious disease and had sent him away to wander in the forest. The Mucky Princess had found him, though, and they had fallen in love and got married. They had gone to live in the princess's land, where she and her pwince, spent their time working the fields, helping the people and getting generally very mucky in the process. But the pwince did not mind; after all, his princess wasn't nicknamed Mucky for nothing.

So there they were, much in love and trying to live happily ever after. But living happily ever after can often be quite difficult, as we shall see.

So, are you sitting comfortably?

Yes?

Well, as I was saying ...

One cold and gloomy winter's afternoon, the Wicked Queen was sitting by the fire, wrapped up in her cloak and shivering with the cold while watching the snowflakes whirling about the mouth of the cave that was now her home.

She could hear loud snoring coming from the back of the cave, which annoyed her so much that she threw a stone into the darkness, hoping to hit the source of the noise. Actually she knew who was making the noise, it was Narvig the Knobbly Gnome of the North, her only companion and loyal friend of the king. She could do nothing that the king would not hear about, as Narvig reported everything she did. Her aim must have been good, because there was a lot of snuffling, and the snoring stopped. Narvig stretched and groaned and shuffled towards the mouth of the cave, sniffing and making some rather bad smells as he went.

"Good morning, your wickedness," he mumbled towards the Wicked Queen, for he was a gnome of few words.

"There's nothing remotely good about it, you vile creature," hissed the Wicked Queen.

Narvig just waved a warty hand at her, made some more bad smells, and sat down just outside the cave. He was not at all bothered by the cold wind and snowflakes.

The Wicked Queen had sat through two long winters like this with only Narvig for company. She had been getting more and more angry while trying to think of a way to escape from the gnome and get her revenge on the king and his family. But try as she might, she had not come up with any ideas that would work. She had thought that she could poison Narvig and then run down the mountain before anyone found out, steal a sword and rush into the palace and strike the king down. But this was just silly. She hadn't got any poison, and the palace guard would stop her long before she got to the king.

No, whatever plan she thought up, when she thought about it again, was not really possible. And so she sat thinking and thinking and with each day becoming more and more wicked. All through those two long winters she had sat and waited for spring, and it was with the coming of the third spring that finally she had a really evil idea.

Outside the cave, in the cracks in the stones, little mountain plants grew. They were tiny. Their flowers were tiny and some had tiny red berries and others had tiny purple berries. Having nothing else to do, she had watched these plants and the birds that came to feed on them. The birds ate all the berries on all the plants except the purple ones and the Wicked Queen wondered why?

There was, she decided, only one way to find out; an experiment, and of course, being wicked, her experiment was very evil.

Now, the Wicked Queen had one other special talent, apart from her wickedness, and that was her patience, and she set about an experiment that would take lots of patience.

The Wicked Queen started to make friends with the small birds by gathering their favourite berries and offering them from between her fingers until after several weeks the birds came to trust her and fed from her hand. At the same time, she gathered the purple berries and hid them in the cave in case Narvig became suspicious. After some time, one bird became so trusting that she was able to close her hand around it and hold it to her like a pet.

Narvig saw this and was surprised, but he just thought that the Wicked Queen had learned her lesson and was becoming a little less wicked.

But he could not have been more wrong.

One day, the Wicked Queen held the little bird to her, went into the cave, and fetched her secret supply of purple berries. The little creature innocently opened its mouth, expecting the Wicked Queen to give it the delicious red berries, but instead the queen dropped the purple berries into the bird's mouth and in moments it was perfectly still. She then hid the tiny creature behind a stone and smiled with satisfaction. At last she had her poison.

But how could she make Narvig eat the berries? The answer came to her a few days later when he was once again snoring at the back of the cave. She went over to him and saw him sleeping on his back, mouth wide open, and snoring loudly.

"So here's a plan," she thought. "But what will I do when I have disposed of the Knobbly Gnome?"

So once again, patiently and wickedly, she plotted and planned very carefully, and when at last she had made her plans, she collected her poison berries and poured them into Narvig's mouth, who spluttered and coughed and swallowed the lot. Then when he had stopped moaning and lay perfectly still, the Wicked Queen let out a yell of triumph and ran away down the mountain as fast as she could.

Clack! Clack! Clack!

CHAPTER TWO

Meanwhile it was springtime and in her kingdom, the Mucky Princess, her pwince and all her people were celebrating at their annual fair. So all were singing and dancing far into the night.

As they walked about the fair, the princess and her pwince smiled and laughed as they remembered the spring three years before, when they had discovered that the pwince did not have a terrible incurable disease, the pony pox. No, it was a spell put on him by his stepmother the Wicked Queen. They remembered how they had tricked her with the magic lipstick and finally revealed the truth and were now living "happily ever after" – or so they thought.

One of their special guests was Martha, the beautician/magician, who had made the magic lipstick that had made all this happiness possible. Martha had set up her tent and a constant stream of visitors had come for their beauty treatment. In the afternoon she hung up her 'CLOSED' sign and went out to enjoy the fair.

She danced and sang until she could dance no more and, exhausted, made her way back to her cottage on the hill behind the stream. She hummed a merry tune as she walked up the path towards her front door and stepped inside, calling for her cat.

"Tiddles! Tiddles," she called but the cat did not appear. "Where are you, you silly cat?"

She called and called, but still Tiddles did not appear. Finally, Martha slumped down in her old chair that stood by the fire. It was a favourite place for the cat.

"Where is that silly cat?" Martha muttered to herself.

"Trusting little fellow, isn't he?" A voice came out of the shadows, making Martha jump out of the chair with fright.

"Who … who is it?" asked Martha, trembling with fear.

A figure in a dark cloak emerged from the shadows holding Tiddles the cat and stroking him roughly.

Martha could not see her face but saw the long white fingers and the bright red nails and knew straight away who it was.

"It's you, but how can it be?" she said.

With that, the Wicked Queen stepped into the light of the fire, threw back her hood and smiled an evil smile at Martha while still keeping a firm hold on the cat.

"Yes, it's me alright," she said while pointing a threatening finger. "And I've got a score to settle with you!"

"You can't scare me," Martha shouted back. "I'm just as good a magician as you, and I'll find a way to counter any spell you can cast."

"That's as may be," replied the Wicked Queen. "But I've got something you haven't got." She smiled her evil smile and stroked the cat menacingly. "You will do exactly as I say or ..." And she held out her hand to show the berries ... "Or these poison berries will make things very bad for Tiddles here."

Martha's heart skipped a beat, and she sighed a huge sigh and slumped back into the chair. "What is it you want of me?" she gasped.

"Well, since you're so good with potions, you can mix one up for me. I want some rouge, some special rouge. Just concentrate carefully while I give you my instructions and remember, I've got little Tiddles here, so no tricks!"

Martha had no choice
and she carefully mixed
powders and potions to
produce the rouge the
Wicked Queen wanted.

"Excellent," she said.
"Now, that wasn't so
difficult, was it? Let's
try a little dab on you."
And the Wicked Queen
rubbed a little of the
rouge into Martha's
cheeks.

Martha felt her cheeks start to burn and glow, but
there was nothing she could do. She could not raise
her arms. She could not move her hands. She couldn't
even nod her head. At least, that is, until the Wicked
Queen gave her commands.

"Now make me a lovely cup of tea, Martha,"
commanded the Wicked Queen, and like it or not,
Martha found herself making tea and bringing it to the
Wicked Queen. "Now," she said, "just pop a couple of
these pretty purple berries into Tiddles' mouth."

Martha did exactly as she was told and watched Tiddles' eyes close and his body slump down weak and helpless.

The Wicked Queen cackled her evil cackle the way evil queens do.

"Now pop a couple into your mouth, Martha," she commanded and the beautician/magician did exactly as she was told. She then collapsed to the floor and lay perfectly still.

"At last, my evil plan is coming together!" she boasted to nobody in particular and with this, took up the pot of rouge and throwing her black cloak and hood about her, swept out through the door and into the fading evening light and made her way to the fair.

The fair was in full swing, and as dusk fell, leaving only firelight to see by, nobody took any notice of another shadowy figure moving through

the fair. The Wicked Queen had timed it just right with just enough light to see by but not enough to be seen by. Without too much trouble, she found Martha's tent, removed the 'CLOSED' sign, lit a candle, and waited for her first 'customer'.

She didn't have to wait long because Martha was a very popular person and soon a young woman came into the tent followed by some friends.

"Hello, Martha," she said, but quickly noticed that it was not Martha at all. "Oh, you're not Martha. Who are you?"

The Wicked Queen had to think quickly and said, "Oh Martha's very tired, so I'm helping out. I'm her cousin ... err ... Queenie. How do you do?" she said and held out her hand.

"Oh, right," said the young woman while nodding, accompanied by lots of 'oohing' and nodding from her friends.

"But there's just one thing," said the Wicked Queen, trying to smile sweetly. "I can only see you one at a time. The treatments are meant to be private." The young woman's friends groaned with disappointment but shuffled out all the same.

"There," said the Wicked Queen.
"Now, what's your name, my dear?" she asked.

"They call me Rosy."

"Oh, that's nice," said the
Wicked Queen, rubbing
her fingers in the pot of
rouge. "Let me give you
some lovely rosy cheeks to
go with your lovely name,"
she said, and cupping
the young woman's face in her hands, she rubbed the
rouge into Rosy's cheeks.

In moments, Rosy was sitting perfectly still and staring
straight ahead. Seeing this, the Wicked Queen ordered
Rosy to: "Fetch your friends in one by one and tell
them what a wonderful thing this rouge is."

And Rosy had no choice but to obey! By morning
there was quite a crowd around the tent with women
and men, young and old, and even some of the palace
guard, all just standing there and looking straight
ahead, still under the spell of the rouge. Inside the
tent, the Wicked Queen awakened after a good night's
sleep with many wicked dreams about ... well, it's best
not to describe them as they really were very wicked.
"Rosy, get in here!" she shouted and Rosy marched
in quickly.

"What can I do for you, your wickedness?"

"Oooh, I'm just tingling with evil," smiled the Wicked Queen, rubbing her hands together. "I just love being called 'your wickedness'. Now go fetch me a cup of tea and a lovely warm croissant with butter and jam."

Rosie obeyed and quickly returned with the Wicked Queen's breakfast, who, when she had finished her meal, rubbed her hands together, went outside to the crowd she had enchanted with her magic rouge and asked: "Now, my slaves, are we all ready for a lovely day of wicked revenge?"

"Yes, we are, your wickedness!" they all shouted back. With this the Wicked Queen marched off at the head of her enchanted followers and towards the palace where the Mucky Princess and her husband the pwince were just getting up.

They both stood by the bedroom window and looked down at the crowd marching towards them, led by a figure in a black cloak.

"What on earth is going on?" said the princess, but the pwince stared hard at the cloaked figure and knew straight away who it was.

"Oh no," he gasped. "It can't be twue. It's my wicked stepmother. How has she escaped?" And with this he shook his head and buried his face in his hands.

CHAPTER THREE

Meanwhile, as the sun began to shine into the mouth of the cave that had been the Wicked Queen's prison for the past three years, the small bird began to awaken from its long, deep sleep.

How can this be? You ask. Surely the little bird had been poisoned. Well, in her hurry to be wicked, the Wicked Queen had not finished her evil experiment. If she had done, then she would have discovered that the poison berries were not poison berries at all but 'berries of enchantment' that simply put those that ate them into a very deep sleep.

The little bird stretched its wings, wriggled its neck and looked about the cave. The fire was out, there was no sign of Narvig, and what was worse, was there was no sign of the Wicked Queen. It was at that moment that he remembered how she had fed him the purple berries and put him into a deep, deep sleep. He knew one thing for certain, the Wicked Queen was as wicked as ever. Why else would she have poisoned him, and with this he flew about the cave looking for Narvig. He quickly found him lying on his back, perfectly still. The little bird lost no time in pecking at Narvig's nose until the gnome awoke with a mighty sneeze that blasted the poor bird across the cold remains of the fire and out of the mouth of the cave.

Outside, the other birds were astonished to see their lost friend, who they thought had been killed, and there was much twittering and bird talk until finally Narvig stumbled outside still half asleep. He looked around confused, as  the flock of birds flew frantically round him. They finally made a formation like an arrow pointing down the mountain. With this, the gnome realised that the fire was out and the Wicked Queen was gone. He did not know what the queen was up to, but he knew it involved some serious wickedness. Without a word – for as you know he was a gnome of few words – he pointed down the mountain and began to run, sending the birds flying ahead to raise the alarm.

Back at the palace, things were looking bad as the Wicked Queen rubbed the Rouge of Revenge into more and more faces and ordered them to make a battering ram to break down the palace doors so that she could get to the Mucky Princess and the pwince.

"Don't wowwy, my dawling," said the pwince, picking up his sword. "I'll defend you!"

"But there are so many of them," she replied. "We are in great danger!"

Which indeed they were, as the great battering ram the Wicked Queen's enchanted army had built, was now thumping against the great oak doors of the palace.

Narvig did not really know what to do as he reached the kingdom. He looked through the trees, with the little birds perched all over him, and he could see the crowds gathered around the battering ram, and the Mucky Princess and her pwince trapped in the tower above.

He reached Martha's cottage and, seeing the door open, went in. He found her siting bolt upright in her chair and staring straight ahead. "Evil magic," he mumbled. "I've got to wake her up." He scratched his knobbles thoughtfully and then, being a gnome, he came up with a simple solution. He walked outside to the well, fetched a large bucket of water and threw it over Martha. This promptly washed off the Rouge of Revenge and Martha awoke spluttering and coughing.

Meanwhile, the birds pecked the cat as hard as they could and eventually it awoke snarling and spitting and clawing the air.

"Oops, sorry, Martha," mumbled the gnome.

"Not at all, you lovely knobbly gnome. We've got to stop that Wicked Queen. She's up to no good, you know."

"I do," replied Narvig, who beckoned her to the door where she could see all the activity at the palace gates.

She gasped in horror and ran back inside the cottage where she began swiftly organising something on her worktable. "Not as clever as she thinks, that Wicked Queen, because while I was mixing up her evil potion, I was also making the antidote!" With this, she spun round, holding a small barrel in one hand and a spray in the other.

"What's that?" enquired Narvig.

"Why, it's the Perfume of Peacefulness. One squirt of this and all the Wicked Queen's powers will disappear. There's no time to lose, my knobbly friend, to the palace!" Martha announced, and with this they swept down the hill with Narvig carrying the barrel full of the Perfume of Peacefulness and Martha the hose. As they approached more closely, they could see the princess and her pwince standing on the balcony and looking very worried indeed.

"Little birds!" roared Narvig in his gruff gnome voice. "Tell the royal couple that we are rushing to their rescue."

The little birds flew about in something of a panic. How could they tell the princess and pwince, when all they could do was ... well ... tweet? But after much tweeting and squawking, they flew off towards the royal balcony and began to fly in formations that each spelled a letter.

H...E...L...P...C...O...M...I...N...G

As they spelled the last letter, Martha and Narvig arrived.

The Wicked Queen had seen them and was standing
on top of the battering ram with her cloak flying,
her ruby red lips shining and her bright red nails
newly painted. She was looking the perfect picture
of evilness.

"Strike them down!" she commanded her 'army'.

But she had not reckoned on Martha's perfume, and
as Martha sprayed the Wicked Queen's bewitched
followers, they stopped, blinked, scratched their heads,
hugged one another and, turning towards the Wicked
Queen, blew her kisses and wished her a peaceful day.

She had fallen silent and stood looking astonished
with her mouth wide open, which was a bad mistake.
When Martha noticed this, she gave her a good squirt
of the Perfume of Peacefulness and the Wicked Queen
swallowed it down. Before long, all of the bewitched
people had been cured and were waving and cheering

the royal couple, who,
as you can imagine, were
very relieved.

In fact, everyone was so
happy, it took a while to
notice the Wicked Queen,
who was sitting on top of
the battering ram smiling
and waving with everybody
else; she was even blowing
kisses to the crowd with
every bit of angry wickedness washed out of her.

The crowd thought this
was marvellous and waved
and smiled back at the
Wicked Queen, but Narvig
was a little worried. He
bent down and whispered
in Martha's ear.

"How long does this
Perfume of Peacefulness
last?" he asked.

"Oh, forever," replied Martha.

And Narvig felt very relieved indeed. He smiled and
grunted the way gnomes do when they feel relieved.

Martha, with a twinkle in her eye, took Narvig by
the hand and they danced the 'Gnomes Knees Up',
the gnomes' dance of celebration, while the little birds
sat on Narvig's knobbles and pecked them with joy
and relief.

The princess and the pwince emerged from the
palace and were carried shoulder high by the crowd,
who promptly dropped the princess in the mud and
made her very mucky indeed. This led to shouts of
"Mucky! Mucky!"

'Just like old times,' thought the princess, who climbed up onto the battering ram and announced that the Spring Fair would go on for an extra day, in celebration. To everyone's astonishment, the Wicked Queen cheered and waved and hugged and kissed the princess. At this, the crowd fell silent, thinking that perhaps the Wicked Queen was up to her old tricks. But no, the Perfume of Peacefulness had done its work and the Wicked Queen was wicked no more.

MUCKY! MUCKY! MUCKY!

So, you're thinking, at last a happy ending. Well, almost. Most of the time, the Wicked Queen was happy and smiling, but sometimes, if the weather was a bit rainy or her favourite football team lost, she could be a bit … well … moany. Even this was alright, though, because the princess took away her title of the Wicked Queen and made her the Duchess of Doom and gave her a very important job.

She was given her very own house next to the royal palace, and if anyone was feeling moany, instead of bothering and annoying their friends and relations with their moaniness, they could visit the Duchess of Doom, completely free of charge, and they would have a good moan together.

THE END
for now...